Diamond Willow

Also by Helen Frost

Diamond Willow

HELEN FROST

SQUARE
FISH

Farrar Straus Giroux
New York

SQUARE
FISH

An Imprint of Macmillan

DIAMOND WILLOW. Copyright © 2008 by Helen Frost. All rights reserved.
Printed in the United States of America by R. R. Donnelley & Sons
Company, Harrisonburg, Virginia. For information, address Square Fish,
175 Fifth Avenue, New York, NY 10010.

Square Fish and the Square Fish logo are trademarks of Macmillan and are used by
Farrar Straus Giroux under license from Macmillan.

Library of Congress Cataloging-in-Publication Data
Frost, Helen, date.
   Diamond Willow / Helen Frost.
      p.   cm.
   Summary: In a remote area of Alaska, twelve-year-old Willow helps her father with
their sled dogs when she is not at school, wishing she were more popular, all the while
unaware that the animals surrounding her carry the spirits of ancestors who care for her.
   ISBN 978-0-312-60383-0
   [1. Spirits—Fiction.   2. Sled dogs—Fiction.   3. Dogs—Fiction.   4. Family life—
Alaska—Fiction.   5. Popularity—Fiction.   6. Schools—Fiction.   7. Athapascan
Indians—Fiction.   8. Indians of North America—Alaska—Fiction.   9. Alaska—
Fiction.]   I. Title.

PZ7.F9205Dia 2008
[Fic]—dc22

                                                                    2006037438

Originally published in the United States by Frances Foster Books, an imprint of
Farrar Straus Giroux
First Square Fish Edition: May 2011
Square Fish logo designed by Filomena Tuosto
Book designed by Nancy Goldenberg
mackids.com

10

AR: 4.3 / LEXILE: 670L

For
Glen,
strong and
brave, whose
eyes shine like
blueberries
in warm
sun.

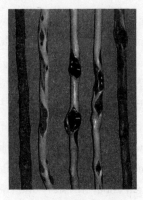

AUTHOR'S NOTE

Diamond Willow takes place in Old Fork, a fictional town of about six hundred people, located on a river in interior Alaska.

There are no paved roads in and out of town; people travel by airplane, boat, snowmachine, and dogsled. They drive around Old Fork in cars, pickups, and four-wheelers, which are brought into town on a barge during the summer months when the river is not frozen.

Willow, the main character, is part Athabascan. Through her mother, she is descended from people who have lived in Alaska for many centuries. Her ancestors on her father's side came from Europe and migrated across Canada and the United States for about 160 years before her father settled in Old Fork.

Most of the story is told in diamond-shaped poems, with a hidden message printed in darker ink at the center of each one. I got this idea from a lamp and a walking stick, both made of diamond willow. The lamp was made by Dr. Irving Preine as a wedding gift for my parents; I remember it from my childhood. As an adult, I lived in Telida, a small Athabascan community in interior Alaska, on the Kuskokwim River, near Mount McKinley. I taught all the students in Telida School, five to ten students in kindergarten through sixth grade. When I left, Deaphon Eluska, the grandfather of two of my students, gave me a diamond willow walking stick that he found near Telida and peeled, sanded, and polished to a beautiful finish. That stick hung in my study as I thought about this story and composed the poems.

Diamond willow grows in northern climates. It has rough gray bark, often crusted with gray-green lichen. Removing the bark and sanding and polishing the stick reveals reddish-brown diamonds, each with a small dark center.

Some people think that diamond willow is a specific type of willow, like weeping willow or pussy willow, but it is not. The diamonds form on several different kinds of shrub willows when a branch is injured and falls away. The dark center of each diamond is the scar of the missing branch.

The scars, and the diamonds that form around them, give diamond willow its beauty, and gave me the idea for my story.

Diamond Willow

7
a.m.
Twenty
below zero,
ribbons of white
and green and purple
dancing in the blue-black sky.
I'm up with Dad as usual, feeding
our six dogs. I climb the ladder to the cache,
toss four dried salmon out to Dad. He watches
me as I back down: *Be careful on that broken rung.*
I pack snow into the dog pot; **Dad** gets a good fire going
in the oil-drum stove. He **loves these dogs** like I do. We're
both out here on weekends, **as much as** we can be, and every
day before and after school. **He loves** Roxy most. *Willow, go*
get the pliers, he says, showing **me** a quill in Roxy's foot.
(It's surprising that a porcupine is out this time of year.)
I bring the pliers; Dad pulls out the quill, rubs in salve;
then we go from dog to dog, spreading fresh straw.
Hey, Magoo. Hey, Samson. Roxy, you stay off
that foot today. Dad pats Prince on the head.
Lucky sniffs my hand—she smells salmon.
I find a bur in Cora's ear and get it out.
The snow melts into water, simmers
in the cooking pot. I drop in the
salmon, add some cornmeal.
The dogs love that smell.
They start to howl
and I howl
back.

I

was

named

after a stick.

The way Mom tells it,

she couldn't get Dad to agree

on any names: Ellen, after Grandma?

Sally, after Dad's great-aunt in Michigan?

No, he wanted something modern, something

meaningful. *It will come to us,* Dad kept saying.

Let's hope it comes before the baby learns to walk,

said **Mom**. ***Always does,*** said Dad. That's how they

argue, each **knows what** they want, but neither seems

to think it **matters** much who wins. Since Mom gives

in before Dad **most** of the time, Dad gets his way a lot.

He told me that just before I was born, he found a small

stand of diamond willow and brought home one stick.

That's it! Let's name our baby Diamond Willow!

Mom had to think about it for a few days.

I can see it now: They're on the airplane

flying to Anchorage. Mom's in labor,

she'll agree to almost anything.

Okay, she says. So Dad puts

Diamond Willow on my

birth certificate, and

then Mom says,

We will call

the baby

Willow.

If
my
parents
had called
me Diamond,
would I have been
one of those sparkly
kinds of girls? I'm not
sparkly. I'm definitely not
a precious diamond—you know,
the kind of person everyone looks at
the minute she steps into a room. I'm the
exact opposite: **I'm skinny**, average height,
brown hair, **and ordinary** eyes. Good. I don't
want to sparkle **like a** jewel. I would much rather
blend in than **stick** out. Also, I'm not one of
those dog-obsessed kids who talk about
nothing but racing in the Jr. Iditarod.
I like being alone with my dogs
on the trail. Just us, the trees,
the snow, the stories I see
in the animal tracks.
No teachers, no
parents, no
sneak-up-
on-you
boys.

In
the
middle
of my family
in the middle of
a middle-size town
in the middle of Alaska,
you will **find** middle-size,
middle-kid, **me**. My father
teaches science in the middle
of my middle school. My mother
is usually in the middle of my house.
My brother, Marty, taller and smarter
than I ever hope to be, goes to college in
big-city Fairbanks. My sister, Zanna (short
for Suzanna), is six years younger and
twelve inches shorter than I am.
She follows me everywhere—
except for the dog yard.
I don't know why
my little sister is
so scared of
dogs.

What
I love
about dogs:
They don't talk
behind your back.
If they're mad at you,
they bark a couple times
and get it over with. It's true
they slobber on you sometimes.
(I'm glad **people** don't do that.) They
jump out and **scare** you in the dark. (I know,
I should say **me**, not "you"—some people aren't
afraid of anything.) But dogs don't make fun
of you. They don't hit you in the back
of your neck with an ice-covered
snowball, and if they did, and
it made you cry, all their
friends wouldn't stand
there laughing
at you.
(Me.)

Three
votes! Did they
have to announce that?
Why not just say, *Congratulations
to our new Student Council representative,
Richard Olenka.* **Why** say how many votes each
person got (12, 7, 3)? I **don't** know why I decided to
run in the first place. A couple **people** said I should,
and I thought, Why not? (I don't **like** staying after
school, and no one would listen to **me** even if
I did have anything to say, which I don't.)
Now here I am, home right after school,
and as soon as we finish feeding
the dogs, Dad says, *Willow,
could you help me clean
out the woodshed?*
I say, *Okay,* but
it feels like
I'm getting
punished
for being
a loser.

We're
cleaning
the woodshed,
and I lift up a tarp.
An old gray stick falls out.
Just a stick. **Why** does it even catch
my eye? *Dad, what* ***is*** *this?* I turn it over in
my hands a few times; **Dad** studies it for a couple
minutes, and then he gets so excited he almost pops.
Willow, let me tell you ***about*** *this! What you have*
found is more than just ***an old*** *stick. This is the*
diamond willow ***stick*** *I found that afternoon,*
just before you were born! Can it be—
let's see—twelve years ago already?
All this time, I thought it was lost.
He hands it back to me like it's
studded with real diamonds.
This belongs to you now.
Use your sharpest knife
to skin off the bark.
Find the diamonds.
Polish the whole
thing. It will
be beautiful,
Dad says.
You'll
see.

I

came

out here to

the mudroom

so I could be alone

and make a mess while I

think my own thoughts and

skin the bark off my stick. But it's

impossible to be alone in this house.

Mom: *Willow, don't use that sharp knife*

when you're mad. I say, *I'm not mad, Mom,*

just leave me alone! and she looks at me like

I proved her point. Then, on my very next cut,

the knife slips and I rip my jeans (not too bad;

luckily, Mom doesn't seem to notice). Maybe I

should go live with **Grandma**. I bet she'd let me

stay out there with her **and Grandpa**. She could

homeschool me. I **think** I'd do better in math if

I didn't worry about how **I'm** going to get a bad

grade while Kaylie gets her **perfect** grades on

every test, then shows me her stupid paper,

and asks how I did, and, if I show her,

offers to help me figure out where

I went wrong, "so you can

do better next time,

Willow."

I
want
to mush
the dogs out
to Grandma and
Grandpa's. By myself.
I know the way. I've been
there about a hundred times
with Dad and Mom, and once
with Marty when he lived at home.
Their cabin is close to the main trail.
I know **I'm not** going to get lost, and I
won't see **a baby** moose or any bears this
time of year. Even if I did, I'd know enough
to get out of the way, fast. But Mom and
Dad don't seem to see it this way. What
do they think will happen? Dad at least
thinks about it: *She's twelve years old;*
it's twelve miles. Maybe we could
let her try. Mom doesn't
even pause for half a
second before
she says,
No

!

Maybe
they'll let me go
if I just take three dogs,
and leave three dogs here for Dad.
I'd take Roxy, of course—she's smart
and fast and she thinks the same way I do.
Magoo is fun. He doesn't have much experience,
but if I take Cora, she'd help Magoo settle down.
Dad would want one fast dog. **I'll** leave Samson
here with him. Lucky might **try** to get loose
and follow me down the trail **again**, like
the last time we left her, but this time
Dad will be here to help Mom
get her back. Prince can be
hard to handle; it will be
easier without him.
If Dad sees how
carefully I'm
thinking this
through, he
might help
convince
Mom.

I
beg
Mom:
Please!
I'd only take
three dogs. You know
I can handle them. You've
seen me. She won't listen. *You*
are not old enough, she says. *Or*
strong enough. I make a face (should
not have done that). Mom starts in: *A moose*
will charge at three dogs as fast as it will charge
at six. A three-dog team can lose the trail, or pull you
out onto thin ice. What if your sled turns over, or you lose
control of the team? (**Mom** really goes on and on once she gets
started.) *Willow, you **could be** alone out there with a dog fight*
on your hands. (Oh, **right**, Mom, like I've never stopped a
dog fight by myself.) When Mom finally stops talking
and starts thinking, I know enough to quit arguing.
She looks me up and down like we've just met,
then takes a deep breath. *You really want to*
do this, don't you, Willow? It takes me by
surprise, and I almost say, *Never mind,*
Mom, it doesn't matter. But it does
matter. I swallow hard and nod.
Mom says, *I'll think about it*
and decide tomorrow.
What if she says
yes?

You
would
trust her
to take Roxy
by herself? Mom
questions Dad. They
don't know I'm listening.
I know my dogs, Dad answers,
*how **they** are with Willow. It's more*
*that I'd **trust** Roxy to take her. Honey, if*
*it's up to **me**, I say let's let her do this.*
I slip away before they see me.
I'm pretty sure they're
going to say yes.
(Yes!)
I go out
and talk to Roxy
and Cora and Magoo.
I think they're going to let us go
to Grandma and Grandpa's by ourselves!
I get out at noon on Friday—it's the end of the
quarter. We'll leave by one, and be there before dark.
We'll have almost two days out there, and come home
Sunday afternoon! Even as **I** let myself say it,
I'm trying not to **hope** too hard.
I know all **I can do** now is
wait. **It** will jinx
it for sure if
I keep on
begging.

Yes,
I have a
wool sweater
under my jacket.
Extra socks, gloves,
and, yes, I have enough
booties for the dogs. I have
my sleeping bag and a blanket,
in case I get stranded somewhere
(which of course won't happen). *Yes,*
I have matches, a headlamp, a hatchet.
Dad keeps adding things to his checklist.
Zanna comes up as close as she dares, keeping
her distance from the dogs, to give me a card she
made for Grandma. It's cute, a picture of an otter
sliding down a riverbank. **Okay**, Dad says, *it looks
like you're all set. I know you **can** do this. Take it
slow.* He keeps on talking as **I** take my foot off
the brake and let the dogs **go**. He might still
be talking even **now**, yelling out last-
minute warnings: *Don't forget to
call us when you get there!
Watch where the trail . . .*
And I can picture Mom,
standing beside Dad,
her arms folded tight,
like she's holding
me, wrapped
up inside
them.

Fox
tracks,
new snow,
red-streaked sky
and full moon rising.
I know **this** trail, know
where it **gets scary**. I know
where it **sometimes** floods and
freezes over. **And I** know Grandma
and Grandpa will **love it** when they hear
the dogs, knowing that it's me mushing
out to see them. I'm almost there.
Can't be more than half an hour
to go. Down this small
hill, past the burned
stumps. There—I
see the light
by their
door.

John, Willow's great-great-grandfather (Red Fox)

Willow saw my tracks and looked around, but I didn't show myself to her. Don't want to take a chance that her dogs would see or smell me, and take off running after me.

Old times, they wouldn't let a girl go off alone like that. I don't like to see it. That's why I followed her, made sure she got to her grandma's house. (Think of it, my little grandchild someone else's grandma now.)

Lots has changed round here since I was Willow's age. Everyone talks that English now, kids go to school all the time, instead of being out here learning to get food. They should think about what happens when those airplanes don't come in. They should teach the kids how to keep warm, how to feed everyone when it stays cold a long, long time. Hungry times could come again, and what will they do then if they don't learn the old ways now?

I wasn't too sure about that man Willow's mother married. When he first came here, he smiled too much, lots of times for no reason—he'd start smiling when he just met someone, before he even got to know them. He'd put out his hand that way they do, smile, say his name, try to make people talk too much. But he turned out okay. He learned how to hunt and fish, made himself some pretty good snow-shoes. That takes patience.

I've been watching him teach Willow how to run the dogs. She's a quiet one. She knows how to listen to those dogs, so they listen to her, too. They're patient with her. Sometimes when she does something wrong—gets their harnesses all tangled up or something—I'm pretty sure I see them barking inside, but those dogs are polite to Willow. They give her a lot of chances. After a while she always gets it right.

I see her through the window now, with her grandpa and grandma. They love that girl; she's safe here. I'll go back upriver to my den.

All
my life,
this has been
my favorite place.
Grandma's beadwork
on the table, Grandpa's furs
stretched out to dry, the smell of
woodsmoke mingling with the smell
of moose meat frying on the stove.
As soon as **I** walk in, I see that
Grandma's **made** a batch of
doughnuts. **It**'s how she
tells me, without
saying much,
she's happy
that I'm
here.

I
tie
the dogs,
and Grandpa
helps me feed them.
We look at Roxy's foot.
I tell Grandpa she had a run-in
with a porcupine. *Oh,* he says, *that nuné.*
It's one of our Indian words. Or, as we say,
Dinak'i. I know some, from bilingual class,
but not as much as Grandpa and Grandma, not
even as much as Mom. **Sometimes**, when we're
dropping off to sleep out here, **I** hear them talking
Dinak'i, chuckling together, and I **feel** a little bit
left out. Not that I would **like** to go back to
the old times I hear the **two** of them talk
about—back when **people** didn't have
TV, computers, telephones, or
snowmachines and airplanes.
I'd miss all those things.
But I like to listen
to their stories.
I know if I try,
I can learn to
understand
them.

Grandpa
gets up first
and makes a hot
birch fire in the stove.
When the house is warm
Grandma makes a pot of coffee
and cooks pancakes. *Grandma,* I ask,
can I move out here and live with you?
I give her all my reasons. Well, most of them.
She looks down at her sewing. ***I do** know what
you mean, Willow. We'd like to **have** you here.*
I'm surprised! I was expecting **some** argument
about my family, or all the **friends** she thinks
I have at school. Then she goes on: *Could
you and your dad take care of all
those dogs if you're here and
he's there? Maybe you
shouldn't split up
a dog team like
that, Willow.
Those dogs
get used
to each
other.*

Early
evening,
snow starts
falling, burying my
tracks from the trail up to
the dog yard and into the house.
Snow covers all the yellow circles
the dogs have made around their houses,
and half buries the firewood stacked outside.
Grandma stands beside me; we're looking out
the window, and she tilts her head the way she does
when she's thinking of a riddle: **Look***, I see something* . . .
She squints her eyes a little. *Someone* **outside** *is wearing
a sheepskin coat.* I look around **and** figure out what
Grandma means: *Over there—I* **see** *snow piled
on top of an old stump.* **Inside** her warm
kitchen, Grandma nods. She
smiles a little. *That's
right, Willow,
that's
it.*

Sunday
morning, the
snow is deep, but
not so much that I can't
make it home. Grandpa and Dad
go out on snowmachines, meeting halfway
to pack the trail. It's time to leave. If I start now, I'll
have plenty of time to get home before dark. I feed the dogs
a little extra, and **Grandma** says, *Here—put this in your pack.*
Smoked salmon! **Looks like** she's feeding me a little extra, too.
Then she gives **me** the mittens she just finished, beaded
flowers on her home-tanned moose skin, beaver fur
around the cuffs. She could sell them for a lot
of money, and she's giving them to me
when it's not even my birthday.
I put them on, put my
hands on her face.
We both
smile.

It's

warm

today,

almost

up to zero. I

see something:

White clouds blow

across the sky. Too bad

I'm out here alone, with

no one but that spruce hen

to tell my riddle to. (It's the dogs'

breath I see, white puffs going out behind

them as they run.) Here comes the halfway point,

where Grandpa met Dad **this** morning. They warned me

about this part of the trail; this **will be** the stretch to watch,

this bumpy part coming up. *Take it **easy** there,* Grandpa said.

Okay, slow down, Roxy. Good, we're past that rough spot,

now we can go as fast as we want. And I love to go fast!

So does Roxy. She looks back at me and I swear

I see her grin. *Let's go!* we tell each other.

Cora and Magoo perk up their ears

as if to say, *Okay with us!*

I knew I could do this.

Hike, Roxy!

Haw!

Jean, Willow's great-great-great grandmother (Spruce Hen)

Oh, my land! Look at this child flying down the trail!

She comes from people who like to keep moving—my family moved across an ocean when I was about Willow's age; her grandfather hitchhiked across Canada the summer he turned twenty; her father came north on the Alcan Highway—on a motorcycle. Now look—when Willow and Roxy get moving together, I don't see any way to stop them.

Usually, I wouldn't want to stop them, or even slow them down. I fly faster than that myself.

But I've seen what's ahead. At the bottom of this hill, just around the curve, a dead tree fell across the trail, not too long after Willow's father went past this morning. Broken limbs are sticking out all over it.

If she were coming from the other direction, she'd see it in time to stop. But from this direction, at the speed she's going, Willow won't have time to stop her dogs.

The
dogs love
going fast as much
as I do. When we come to
the curve at the bottom of the hill
I'll slow them down a little. But not yet—
this is too much fun! Here's the curve. *What?*
Whoa! Easy, Roxy! I brake hard, the dogs stop—
but not fast enough. Roxy's howl cuts through me.
I set the snow hook, run to her—as fast as I can
through the deep snow. I stumble; a branch
jabs into my leg. *Oww!* **It's my** own
voice I hear, like the **fault** line
of an earthquake, with
everything breaking
around it. Roxy
sticks her face
in the snow.
The snow
turns
red.

Roxy,
look at me.
I hold her head
and stare at her face.
She's bleeding from her eyes
and she won't stop yelping. **I** pull the
tarp off the sled—oh, I **don't** believe this!
I kept saying, *Dad, I **know** I have everything!*
But I didn't bring **the first** aid kit! I don't have
any bandages, or any**thing** like a dog bag to carry
Roxy in the sled. I'm **about** two hours from home.
It's too far to turn back. **This** is serious. *Hush, Roxy.*
I'll think of something. My shirt. It's clean enough.
No one's around, and I won't freeze to death while I
take it off and put my sweater and jacket back on.
Okay. I think I can do this. I have to. *Roxy,*
just let me hold this on your eyes. Please
trust me. Thank you, Roxy. Good dog.
There, I finally stopped the bleeding.
Now, I have to get her in the sled.
I can lift her. But how can I
keep her from shivering
in this bitter
wind?

I
kick the
side of the sled.
How could I be so
stupid? Dad will kill
me! *Calm down, my dear.*
Weird—it seemed like I heard
those words. I look around: Who
said that? All I see is a spruce hen
sitting on a low branch just ahead,
quietly preening her feathers. I watch
her for a minute, **take** a few long, deep
breaths, let my **heart** slow down a little,
and then it comes to me: *Feathers—use
my down sleeping bag.* I manage to get
Roxy into it and strap her to the sled.
I give the dogs some of my smoked
salmon and eat some myself.
(Thank you, Grandma!)
*Cora—you'll have to
lead us home. I'm
counting on
you.*

Jean, Willow's great-great-great grandmother (Spruce Hen)

By the time they pull into the yard, the sun has set behind the mountains. Willow's mother and her father and her sister, Zanna, all run out to meet her. Her mother is all smiles; Zanna's jumping up and down.

Her father looks at Roxy in the sled.

Before he has a chance to say a word, Willow's mother takes her daughter in her arms and pulls her close.

Willow's shoulders start to shake. Her mother makes a gesture to her father: *You take care of Roxy. I'll take care of her.*

My
leg is
bruised
pretty badly.
Mom says it's lucky
I didn't get hurt worse.
*We **shouldn't** have let you go.*
*At least, **someone** should have gone out*
*this afternoon to **be** sure you were okay.* It sounds
like Mom is **mad at** Dad or herself, but not sure which.
She fusses over **me**, covering me with a warm blanket,
making me hot chocolate, telling Zanna to turn
down the TV so I can rest. She doesn't
say a word about Roxy. When Dad
comes in, they go into their
bedroom to talk. I want
to hear what Dad
has to say, but
he doesn't
seem to
want
me
to.

Roxy's
eyes have
always been so
beautiful—deep,
clear brown. Intelligent.
I call it dog-love, that way
she looks at us. Now her eyes
are crusted with—with **what**? They're
all bandaged, and when I lift **a** corner of the
bandage, I see a bloody **mess**. When Dad took her
to the vet, he didn't even ask me to go along! And now
he hasn't told me what she said. He was silent when he
brought Roxy in and made her bed beside the stove.
Dad's not exactly accusing me out loud, but
everything he does says, *Willow,*
how could you? I trusted you!
Roxy was our best dog.
You knew that.
Yes, Dad—
I knew
that.

I
don't
get up early
like I usually do.
I stay in bed when Dad
gets up to feed the dogs. Mom
comes in to see how I'm doing, and
I say, *Mom, I think I better stay home
from school today.* **I can't** *walk
too well.* Her **face** tells me
she'll tell **Dad** for me,
but she's not sure
I'm telling
the entire
truth.

Dad

changes

Roxy's bandage and

makes sure she's comfortable

before he goes to work. After he's gone,

I go in to see her. She can't see me, of course,

but she whimpers when **she** hears me coming, so I

kneel down beside her. I **might** cry, and I don't want her

to hear me do that. I'll try to **be** as brave as she is. *Oh, Roxy,*

*I'm sorry! I knew that **blind** curve was coming up.*

I should have slowed down sooner.

Roxy licks my face,

sniffs my leg

where I'm

hurt,

too.

I

know

Kaylie must be

wondering where I am.

At 11:48, when we have lunch, she

calls from school. (We always eat together.)

Willow, what happened? Your dad said you got hurt!

I don't want to hear about my dad right now. All the kids

think he's so great—they can't wait to get to eighth grade and have

him for science. I'm dreading that. What if he gets mad at me at home,

and then at school **I** have to sit through science class with him? *Thanks,*

Kaylie, but you don't **need** *to feel sorry for me.* I say, *What Dad meant*

was, Roxy got hurt. **You** *know—his favorite dog? He's had her since I*

was Zanna's age! Oh, **Kaylie,** *he's been training her for . . . forever,*

to be his lead dog! And now I think she's blind! Nobody

will say so, but her eyes are all bloody and gross!

Kaylie interrupts: *What about you, Willow?*

What happened to your leg? Why

aren't you here today? I don't

have anyone to sit with.

She's good at changing

the subject. *Sit with*

Richard, I suggest.

Make someone

happy.

Dad
comes home
right after school
and goes straight to Roxy.
I go to my room and close the door.
Willow, he calls to me, but **I can't** tell if he's
going to get mad (*Willow,* **get out** *here and look*
at the once-beautiful eyes **of** *my best dog*) or be nice
(*Please, can we talk about* **this***?*). Probably, he's mad.
Who wouldn't be? Zanna comes in and sits on the
edge of her bed, looking at me like, *Boy, are you*
in big trouble. I start to say shut up, but at the
last second I realize she didn't actually say it.
After a while, Mom knocks. I let her in; she
sits beside me, asks if she can see my leg.
It's not too bad, I say. I roll up my jeans
so I can show her where the bruise has
turned some ugly shade of purple-
brown. She touches the swollen
place with her cool fingers.
Bad enough, she says.
And here's what's
so great about
my mom:
that is
all she
says.

I

can't

avoid Dad

forever. We do live

in the same house together,

after all. When Mom calls me

for dinner, I take a deep breath and go

out to the kitchen. Dad's with Roxy, and I

don't look at either of them. Well, I try not to.

Dad calls me over. *Can we talk about this, Willow?*

He's looking at Roxy's **face**, not mine. *Shall I tell you*

what the vet said? he asks. **It** isn't really a question, and

I can't exactly say, *No, Dad, don't tell me.* I just shrug.

Dad says, *Roxy is blind. There's nothing they can do.*

The exact two sentences I do not want to hear. I know

I should say I'm sorry. I try, but the words get stuck.

I turn away from Dad and Roxy. Mom lays her arm

across my shoulder for a second, and I twist out

from under it, heading for the door. *Sit down*

and eat, now, Willow, Mom says, so I sit

down, but I can't eat. I stare at my plate

and push some beans from one side

to the other. Nobody but Zanna

says much of anything

the whole entire

meal.

Isaac, Willow's great-grandfather (Mouse)

Willow didn't leave me anything tonight. But I can always count on Zanna to start talking with her hands, and drop a lot of crumbs on the floor.

After both girls leave the room, I scurry out to get those crumbs. I'm under the table when I hear their parents talking.

No one shrieks, *A mouse! A mouse!* and jumps up on a chair. (Why do they do that, anyway? They're so big and we're so small.) They're too caught up in their conversation to even notice me.

My ears perk up when Willow's mother asks her father, *Are you going to have Roxy put to sleep?*

He doesn't answer right away.

I don't know, he finally says. *I hate to see her like this.* When he was a child, he couldn't stand to see an animal suffer. Once he found a nest of baby mice whose mother was caught by an owl. He brought them in and fed them. When they were big enough, he took them back where he found them and let them go. The way I heard it, all but one survived.

The vet bill for her eyes could be over a thousand dollars, he says.

Her mother answers, *Yes, that's true. We'd go into debt again.*

But that's not how we should decide, her father says. *Roxy won't* ever pull a sled again, and I've never seen a dog that loves to run like she does. What kind of life will she have?

Her mother thinks about that. *Could she be a house dog? Maybe she'd help keep the mice down.* (That's funny—who's afraid of a blind dog? Roxy would never catch us, even if she could see.)

It's hard to imagine Roxy being happy as a mouser, her father answers.

Her mother nods. *Should we ask Willow to help us decide?* she asks.

I don't think so. She already feels responsible for this, and if we decide to have Roxy put to sleep, I don't want her to feel responsible for that, too.

They're both quiet until her mother says, *It sounds like you've decided.*

Her father looks at the floor and doesn't answer. I keep still. He doesn't see me.

Willow will not like this.

How can I let her know?

I'm

sitting

in a corner

of the kitchen

after everyone has

gone to bed. Roxy's finally

asleep. I'm sanding the diamond

willow stick with all my might, working

on one diamond, trying to find its deep-down

center, thinking, **What** *would it be like to be blind?*

I hear something . . . What **is** it, scuffling under the table

just a few feet away from **this** chair? I'm completely quiet,

and a brown mouse comes **all** the way out into the room, stops

and looks right at me. I'm **about** to tell myself to leave it alone;

it isn't bothering me—maybe it thinks my sawdust is bread crumbs.

But then it does something odd: it climbs up on the telephone table!

I get up to shoo it away. We don't like the mice to chew up paper

for their nests, and this one has its feet on a piece of paper.

I pick up the paper, and it runs off. Brave little thing.

It actually tilts its head and looks at me. (Or did I

imagine that?) I glance down at the paper:

Old Fork Veterinary Services.

"Prognosis." "Options."

"Probable outcome."

"Recommendation:

1. Euthanasia . . ."

Does that mean

what I think

it does?

Here's
what it says
in the dictionary—
"Euthanasia: 1. The act
of killing a person painlessly
for reasons of mercy. 2. A painless
death." It says "person" but I bet it means
dogs, too. How do **they** know it's painless?
Or merciful? Roxy **can't** even talk! How
can someone decide to **kill** someone else
without asking? Does **Roxy** get a vote?
Do I? I can't believe they're even
thinking about this! How can
I stop them? *Come on, Roxy,*
you sleep in my room
tonight. I'll figure
this out in the
morning.

I

know

Dad's the one

who took Roxy to the vet,

but I bet anything Mom's in on it.

From the way they don't look at me

when I bring Roxy back into the kitchen,

I can see they aren't going to ask my opinion.

I pick up the paper from the vet, wave it at them.

*I found **this**,* I tell them. *I know what euthanasia is.*

*This **means** you're going to kill Roxy, doesn't it?* Dad

looks at Mom. **It's** so obvious they think this is one of

those grown-**up**, don't-tell-the-children conversations.

*Willow, listen **to me**,* Dad says. Okay, I'm listening.

Even for us, this is a hard thing to decide.

See? That's what I mean:

"even"!

So
who
besides me
is on Roxy's side?
Grandma and Grandpa
would take care of her, I know it!
But **how can I** get Roxy out to them?
I need someone to **hold on to her** in the sled
while I mush the other dogs. If only Marty
would come home. If only Zanna were
a few years older, and not such
a little blabbermouth.
There has to be
someone . . .
Kaylie?

I

have to

plan this exactly.

If Kaylie and I leave school

right at 11:50, we'll get home just as

Mom leaves to take Zanna to kindergarten.

This is the day she volunteers in Zanna's class,

so we'll have time to pack the sled, hitch the dogs,

and leave for Grandma and Grandpa's house by 1:00.

We can be on the trail for two hours before anyone notices

we're gone, and if all goes well, we can get there before dark.

I find Kaylie beside her locker. *It's an emergency!* I tell her.

*Please! You have to meet me at **the** back door of the school.*

*Don't say anything to anyone. Come **right** after math class.*

She wants me to explain every**thing**, but there's no time.

It will be really hard to get her **to do** this. *Bring your coat*

and boots, I add. She stares at me. *Please, Kaylie, it's a*

matter of life and death, I beg. It sounds so dramatic,

but Kaylie has had perfect attendance since third

grade, and I need her to skip an afternoon of

school without telling her mom, and she's

one of those people who tells her mom

everything. If we can just get Roxy

out there where she's safe, I know

tomorrow morning Grandpa

will bring Kaylie back on

his snowmachine, and

I'll mush home.

It has to

work.

We

meet

like we

planned. I don't

go by Dad's classroom

on the way to meet Kaylie

with my coat on, **so** nobody asks

any questions about **what** I'm doing. Kaylie

could have slipped out, too, **if** Richard didn't have

such a major crush on her. **We** try to distract him with a

not-quite-lie: *We're going to **get** lunch at my house today.*

Kaylie's nervous. She has been **grounded** exactly once in her

life, almost two years ago now, **for** something like seven hours,

and she still talks about that. **This** might be the worst thing she's

ever done. I fill her in on the details of my plan as we walk home

the back way, so neither of our moms will see us. *But, Willow,*

Kaylie says, *I've never mushed dogs before.* It's true, but she

loves animals. *All you have to do is sit in the sled with Roxy,*

keep her calm, and make sure her eyes are protected from

the wind. She's still trying to decide when we get home,

just as Mom drives off with Zanna on the snowmachine.

Perfect timing. When we go inside, Roxy comes right

over to Kaylie, wagging her tail, and I'm sure I see

them smile at each other. I find a note on

the telephone table, Mom's writing:

"Vet—3:45. Bring blanket

to wrap body. Tell the

children? Okay,

if old enough to

understand."

Emma, Kaylie's great-grandmother (Chickadee)

Oh, for heaven's sake, what are those girls up to now? I see that spruce hen waiting over there, ready to fly along with Willow. I suppose I'll do the same for Kaylie. Sometimes she puts seeds on her mitten and holds it out to me. *Chic-a-dee-dee,* she says; I believe it's her way of trying to talk to me. I like that. I hop right up on her hand and take the seeds, then fly off to a nearby tree to eat them. Kaylie keeps an eye on me. I keep an eye on her.

I don't like the looks of this one bit—that dog should be inside where it's warm and dry. The girls should be in school where they belong. Don't they see that stormy sky? Do their parents know what they're up to?

It looks like they have Roxy well wrapped in a dog bag and a warm blanket. Cora, Lucky, and Magoo seem eager to start out. Willow does know how to handle dogs, I'll say that for her. If only she weren't quite so headstrong. She gets these crazy ideas and pulls Kaylie along like this. I never know quite what will happen.

I'm

not sure

about this

weather. It's

that kind where

first there's **a** pocket of

sharp cold, then a **little** farther on

the air gets warm. The **snow** comes down

and stops and starts again—I **won't** quite say so,

but I'm kind of nervous. Roxy is **hurt**—I can't turn back!

We have to keep moving in case **anyone** comes and tries to stop us.

When Mom gets home, she'll call Dad, who **will** figure out what I'm doing.

He'll start after me on his snowmachine. Now **it** looks like Kaylie's scared;

she keeps glancing over her shoulder at the sky behind us. When we stop

to rest the dogs, she takes out some seeds and holds them on her

mitten. A chickadee comes right down and grabs one, then

flies on ahead of us. Kaylie watches it. *Come on,* she says,

we should hurry, Willow. What if the snow gets worse,

so your grandpa can't bring me back? We're more

than halfway there, so I'm not too worried,

but she's right about the weather.

It's snowing harder than

it was just a few

minutes

ago.

Where
is the fork
in the trail?
Shouldn't we
have come to it
by now? Snow
is coming down
so fast and hard I
can barely see. And
why is Roxy whining?
Her eyes are bandaged;
she couldn't know if we
missed the fork back there.
Could she? **I'm not** going to
turn back. I'm pretty **sure** if we
keep going for **about** ten more
minutes on **this** trail, we'll come
to the fork. If not, we'll have to
go back to see if we can find it.
Mom and Dad are definitely
home by now. It's starting
to get dark, and Cora
doesn't know the
way like Roxy
did. Like
I was so
sure I
did.

We've
been back and forth
on this same stretch of trail three
times now—I still can't find the fork.
Blinding snow swirls ahead of us, behind us,
and it's getting colder and darker by the minute.
Now Kaylie thinks we should **try** to go back home.
She doesn't know I'm **not** sure where we are.
I don't know which way **to** go from here
to get home. I taste **panic** rising
in my throat. I swallow it.
And then a spruce hen
bursts out, right
in front of my
face. *Do I*
know
you?

The
spruce
hen flies to a
low branch, and
comes to a **stop** at the
point **where** the branch
slopes down. ***You are*** *starting*
to shiver, Kaylie says. ***You might*** *be getting*
hypothermia. We need to warm up. ***Be*** *sensible, Willow.*
Who made her the mother? But it's true. ***All right****, I agree,*
we might as well make a fire here and wait for the snow to stop.
Kaylie looks around, then stares at me. We both know this kind
of snow could fall all night. We start to search for dry firewood,
and beneath the spruce tree's low, snow-covered branches,
we find a shelter. *Kaylie, look,* I say, *we can cut spruce*
boughs for the floor, and lean the sled on its side
to shield us from the wind. Help me
get Roxy in here. Be careful
not to knock the snow
off that branch.
I think the
three of us
can fit in
here.

At
least
we brought
the survival kit.
And extra salmon to give
Grandma and Grandpa for Roxy.
We got a fire going; we melted snow.
We boiled water and checked Roxy's eyes.
We changed her bandage. We kept her warm.
We cooked a pot of salmon stew, gave plenty
to the dogs. Now **we can** eat some stew
ourselves. *Let's not **think** of this as*
"We're eating dog food."
We agree:
We're all in this
*together; **we're** sharing food*
*with four **good** dogs.* We try not to think
about the **people** who are worrying about us.
We aren't sure if it's safe for us to go to sleep—
if it gets colder, we could freeze to death out here.
One thing we know for sure: if we can stay alive
until tomorrow, when we do get home,
we can look forward to being
in the worst trouble
either of us
has ever
been
in.

Here's
what I see
when I light
my candle: Kaylie in her
dark green sleeping bag, her back
against the sled; me in my sleeping bag, curled
around Roxy in her dog-bag, spruce boughs under us,
a red blanket over us. Nearby, in a snow cave we hollowed out,
we hear Lucky breathing. Magoo whimpers in his sleep and Cora
snores a little. The spruce tree seems like **it's** as wide awake as I am,
spreading her branches to make this **cold**, cozy shelter. If I can't stay
awake all night, I'll wake up Kaylie, **and** she'll stay awake while I
sleep. I won't disturb her just because **I'm scared**. I'm the one
who dragged her into this. As long as everyone is breathing,
I'm pretty sure we'll be okay. It's still snowing
just as hard as it was
before.

Jean, Willow's great-great-great grandmother (Spruce Hen)

I'm roosting under the other side of this tree, awake with Willow, though she doesn't see me. Do I hear something? Yes, it's the sound of someone tearing through the forest on one of those noisy things they ride on. I'll fly out and see what I can see.

The snow has finally let up a little, but the wind keeps blowing it around. The dogsled tracks are completely covered.

There's the noisy thing, moving faster than I've ever seen one move at night.

Ah, yes—it's Willow's father driving it. His headlight shines ahead on the trail that Willow couldn't find. If her ears are sharp, and if she can remember the direction of the sound, it could help her find the right trail tomorrow morning.

Now her father has arrived at her grandparents' house—they've kept a light on for him. No one is asleep tonight. I watch them through the window as they sit and talk. Her father drinks three cups of coffee, then heads out into the night again, more slowly this time. At the fork, he stops and looks around, examining both trails for tracks, but there's nothing he can see.

Willow never got that far. She took a wrong turn before the fork and got lost on an old trail no one ever uses anymore. Her father slows down when he passes it, as if he's thinking. It would be a hard trail to travel in the dark.

Do I hear . . . ? Yes, the dogs are howling. Good job, Willow. If her father stops, he'll hear them—but is there any way to stop him?

I swoop in close and he looks up.

What was that? he says out loud. *Too small to be an owl.*

I try again. He slows down a little, but he doesn't stop. He shakes his head and goes on home.

I

hear a

snowmachine!

I shake Kaylie: *Wake up!*

Come on, we have to make noise!

She half opens her eyes, pushes Roxy,

and says, ***I wish** you wouldn't sit so close to me,*

Richard. **I could** tease her about it, but I don't. *I saw*

*the spruce hen **fly** off in that direction about an hour ago*

and I thought I heard a snowmachine, but I wasn't sure.

It went past, and everything was quiet. Now there it is

again. Our parents must be out looking for us, Kaylie.

She says, *I don't know. Out on a snowmachine in the*

middle of the night? That's crazy. That's not even

the direction of the trail we came on, is it? She's

wide awake now. *Let's wake up the dogs,* I say,

get them howling loud enough so whoever is

out there will hear us. We start howling

and the dogs raise their voices too.

The snowmachine doesn't stop.

It's moving farther away.

We stop howling, and

silence closes in.

It's darker than

before. I can't

seem to get

warm.

Willow,
you sleep now,
Kaylie says. *I'll stay*
awake. We're not freezing.
I trust her to wake me up if . . .
If what? That's what I don't know.
I lie **down** with Roxy and doze off.
Then, **deep** in her throat, Roxy growls,
and **I'm** wide awake. Her ears perk up.
Is Roxy **scared**? Should we be? Kaylie
says, *Want to make another fire? We*
*could freeze to **death** out here.* We
make a small fire, but we don't
want to go out in the dark
to get more firewood.
What did Roxy
hear?

Out
here in
the middle of
the long cold night,
under the snow-covered
spruce tree, Kaylie and Roxy
and I lie awake, keeping each other
warm. Like a steady **heart**beat, Kaylie
speaks a few words **to** me and I answer.
The night has a **heart**beat of its own,
and somehow **we're** inside it. Kaylie
says, *When I **held** Roxy in the sled,*
it seemed like she was watching
where we were going, even
though she's blind. I know
just what Kaylie means.
Willow, she whispers,
I'm scared. Are you?
I don't try to deny it.
Maybe a little, but
look—it's almost
morning. Roxy
sniffs at the
first hint of
light, and
stretches.

It's

morning,

and Roxy's eyes

are no worse than they were

last night. *I think I know where we*

went wrong, I say. *If I'm right, it won't be hard*

to find our way back to that trail and take it to my

grandparents' house. Kaylie says, *No way, Willow. We're*

going home. (Not me, I'm not giving up. But I don't argue yet.)

We feed the dogs, pack the sled, hitch up Cora, Lucky, and Magoo,

and start down the trail, heading in the direction of the snowmachine

we heard. It's so much easier to find our way this morning. But—

what are these big tracks? *Look,* **we have** *a lynx around here!*

We study the tracks, trying **to** figure out which way it went.

Kaylie says, *Let's get going.* **Save all this talk for later.**

So we set off together. But I look at **Roxy**, thinking:

She warned us, maybe scared off a lynx that came

too close. We thought we were taking care of

her, and all the time she was taking care

of us. *Hike, Cora! Hike, Magoo!*

All right, Lucky! It's time

to be on our way—

to Grandma's

house.

We

have to

go about a mile

on the wrong trail before

we come to the right one. I see

what happened: Cora hasn't been

to Grandma and Grandpa's house as often

as Roxy has. She made a wrong turn down the

old trail. The snow was falling so hard by then, we

couldn't see past the dogs. That's why we didn't notice

we were headed in the wrong direction—everything is

so clear this morning. Hey! Is that **what** I think it is?

*Kaylie, look! I think the lynx **was** here not long ago.*

All around the intersection of **the** old trail and the

new one, we see tracks of a large **lynx**, fresh this

morning. We both sink in **up to** our knees,

but the lynx walked on top of the snow

no more than an hour ago, I bet.

The fork we should have

come to yesterday

can't be much

farther now.

This time

I know

I'll

see

it.

I
can't
believe this!
Kaylie is stressing out
about missing half a day of
school! She wants to go home
instead of keeping on and trying to
get Roxy to Grandma and Grandpa's.
We're almost there! **I'm** afraid one of
our dads is coming, **not** far behind us.
I know we're **giving** everyone a scare.
Maybe they've been **up** all night, but
we still have to keep going! Listen!
I hear dogs on the trail behind us.
At least it's not a snowmachine.
If it's Dad, he'll have Prince and
Samson. They aren't as fast as
these three dogs, but his sled
will be lighter than ours—
he could catch up. *Hike,*
Cora! Good job, Lucky!
Roxy barks twice, like
she's cheering us on.
Magoo barks, too,
and then even
Kaylie yells,
Go!

Look!

Where?

What is it?

An animal . . .

a streak of gold.

Roxy growls deep

in her throat, like she did

in the middle of the night.

We slow down and stare into

the forest—the lynx stares back

at us. When we move on and speed

up, so does it. **It's sleek**, graceful,

moving beside us **and** keeping up.

I know we're **strong** enough

to outrun it if we want to,

but I don't think

I want

to.

Albert, Richard's grandfather (Lynx)

There's no doubt about it—Richard is smitten with this Kaylie. I remember being thirteen and in love. The girl's name was Celina, her hair was black, her laugh reminded me of northern lights. I'd try anything to make Celina laugh. She paid me no more mind than Kaylie pays to Richard, but I couldn't help myself. I wanted to protect her—whether or not she wanted my protection. Or so I told myself. Truth was, I just wanted to be near her.

Yesterday, when word went out that the girls were missing in the blizzard, Richard strapped on his snowshoes and headed down the trail. He would have loved to find those girls—especially Kaylie—and help them get to safety. But the storm grew worse, and he turned back—the boy does have some sense.

I went out to see what I could see.

That dog they call Cora (I knew her as Mary; as I recall, she was Willow's grandpa's auntie) can remember when the old trail was the only trail. It didn't surprise me to see her lead them that way, but I was afraid it would mean trouble. I decided to follow and stay with them.

Roxy doesn't miss much—she heard me in the night and growled, so I moved on. The snow had stopped by then. I left a few tracks for them to find this morning, and a few more by the trail where they took the wrong turn yesterday.

This morning, before the crack of dawn, Richard hitched up his four dogs and came out looking for the girls. If he'd left home a little earlier, he would have seen my tracks before they did; he might have met them as they came back down the old trail. But Willow and Kaylie passed that place before he got there. He's on the trail behind them now. His sled is almost empty, so he's moving faster than they are. He may yet be of some use.

As for me, I'm teasing them a little. Willow doesn't mind if I run along beside them, and if Kaylie is a little scared, well, that will give Richard something to protect her from.

If

we go

too fast,

we could

have another

accident. If we

don't go fast enough,

the dogs behind us will

catch up. They're getting close.

I hear a musher's voice, but I can't tell

for sure if it's Dad. **Kaylie is** holding Roxy

securely in the sled. There's **a good** trail packed down

just right. (Thank you, whatever **friend** we heard in the middle

of last night, out on a snowmachine, packing the trail for us.)

Okay—I'm going to go a little faster, be as careful as I can.

If the trail is good all the way to Grandma and Grandpa's,

we can make it in another fifteen minutes. If it's Dad

behind me, we might be able to get there before he

catches up. Kaylie turns around in the sled so she

can watch the trail behind us. Whoever it is,

they're getting closer—it sounds like

they have more than two dogs.

What! Kaylie almost falls

out of the sled—

Richard?

Kaylie

and Richard

are ridiculously

happy to see each other.

The lynx comes to the edge

of the trees to look out at us. Richard

roars at it, making this wild face. Kaylie

laughs. Just before the lynx runs off, it gives

the two of them a look—is it chuckling at them?

I hold the two dog teams apart and keep Roxy quiet.

Richard wants to take Kaylie home. ***Don't you know how***

worried people are? If she does **leave** to go with him, what

will I do without anyone to hold **Roxy**? It's Kaylie's choice,

and I can't stop her. She looks at Roxy **and me**. She asks,

Could you take Roxy the rest of the way **alone**? I think

so—I'm almost there. If they go back, they can tell

Mom and Dad I'm okay. Kaylie will miss only

half a day of school. *Sure,* I say. I turn away.

I tuck our two sleeping bags around Roxy.

I'll be fine. Go ahead. Roxy whines

a little as we watch them go.

I put my arms around her.

Snow falls from a

branch onto her

face and mine.

I brush it

off.

All
my doubts
come circling in
as soon as I'm alone.
It's like I'm a mouse and
they're hawks that have been
watching, out of sight, and now
they see their chance to swoop down
on me. What if Roxy gets worse from
being on this trip? **She** needs her bandage
changed, and she **has to stay** warm and dry.
Kaylie and I kept her **with us** in the shelter
all night, but I know she should have been
indoors. I didn't even leave Mom and Dad
a note—I couldn't think of what to say
that wouldn't make them mad, so I
just left without saying anything,
which will make them madder.
And there's this problem:
Grandma and Grandpa
might say no. What if
they already have
too many dogs,
and can't
keep our
Roxy?

Oh,

Roxy,

look at you,

keeping your head tucked

down in the sled, so the cold wind

won't hurt your eyes. **I love** how your right

ear perks up like that. What do **you** hear? Dogs barking?

Maybe Grandpa's. (*Come on,* ***Roxy****, we're waiting for you!*)

I love how, when we first hear the *thwack* of Grandpa's ax,

you lift your head a little and turn to me, like you used to

when you could see. It's early for Grandpa to be out

chopping wood. I bet he's been up all night,

waiting for us. Now we're almost there.

Grandma and Grandpa will feed us.

No one will get mad. They'll

take care of you, Roxy.

I know they will.

They have

to.

Here

is what is

so great about

Grandma and Grandpa:

They don't ask a single question

until Cora, Lucky, and Magoo are tied

and fed, and **I'm inside** wearing dry clothes,

too big, but clean **and warm, and** Grandpa has

brought Roxy in so she's **safe**, too, and now she's

eating beaver soup, and someone must have changed

her bandage and Grandma puts a plate of pancakes

in front of me and fried moose meat and potatoes.

I'm more hungry than I have ever been in my life.

I finish eating and slump in my chair, and then

Grandma picks up her sewing and says,

Willow, you want to talk—even

then it's not exactly

a question. *Yes,* I

say, *I want*

to talk.

To you.

About

Roxy.

See,

I say.

I struggle

for words and

Grandma listens

with her hands and ears

and eyes, and that's exactly

what I want to tell her, how Roxy

does that, too. **Grandma**, *Roxy doesn't*

*need her eyes—she still **sees me***. *Or maybe she*

knows me without seeing. She trusts us! How can

Dad and Mom just let her go? I can't let them do that.

So I brought her here to you. If you can keep her, I'll

bring food for her. I'll come out every weekend and

brush her coat. When her eyes are better, I'll take

her out and let her run. Grandma doesn't

answer for the longest time, and I try

to think of something else to say,

but I can't, so I just stop.

Grandma looks at me,

she looks at Roxy.

Finally, she says,

Maybe this dog

doesn't want

to stay with

us. I bet

she wants

to stay

with

you.

Jean, Willow's great-great-great grandmother (Spruce Hen)

What's become of Kaylie and Richard (and Albert, that old lynx)? Let me see what I can see.

There they are. Richard's dogs are well behaved. He lets Kaylie drive them for a while, standing on the runners in front of him, so happy, like she's forgotten all about the mischief she's been making, the trouble she'll be in when she gets home.

I fly to the place where the old trail meets the new trail. It looks like half the town is here, reading the tracks in the snow.

They went this way, down the old trail, says Kaylie's mother.

No, that's where they came from, Willow's dad points out. *Then they turned this way . . . Look.*

Little Zanna is walking around by herself, off to the side. *What's this big track? Kind of like a cat, only bigger.*

Lynx! says Willow's mother. *I haven't seen a lynx around here for thirteen years!*

Prince and Samson look down the trail and bark. Everyone looks up.

Listen! Willow's father says. *Dogs in the distance . . . coming this way. Willow and Kaylie!*

When Richard and Kaylie come down the trail, everyone stares at them like Kaylie is a ghost and Richard has brought her back to the land of the living.

Now listen to them, all talking at once. I've never seen so much hugging and handshaking. It looks like Richard is meeting Kaylie's parents for the first time—he has that proud I-saved-your-daughter look. If Kaylie is in trouble, her parents forget to tell her. Everyone stops talking and lets her tell her story.

Soon everyone but Willow's family heads back into town.

I
hear
something,
Grandma says.
Our snowmachine!
Dad's driving it, fast.
Even though I'm glad he's
here, and **I know I'm** lucky to be
alive, I'm still **a little** scared. But when Dad
comes in, it is **amazing**—he is way, way
more happy to see me than he is mad
about what I did. He comes in and
hugs me hard, for a long time.
His first question takes me by
surprise: not, *How is Roxy?*
but, *How is your leg?* I
haven't thought about
it since yesterday. *Fine,*
I say, and I realize it's
true. After a while, I
hear Mom coming
with the dogs. She
doesn't really like
dog-mushing, but
she can do it when
she has to. Zanna
is fast asleep in
the sled, so
warm, so
safe.

They've
already heard most
of the story from Kaylie:
the blinding snow, the wrong trail,
the shelter under the spruce tree. And Zanna
found the lynx tracks, so they know about that.
What's left for me to say? I know I have to tell
them **I'm** sorry, and I am, and I do. But Roxy
is **older than** Zanna! Part of the family!
Shouldn't **they** be a little sorry, too?
Why did they **think** it was
okay to make such a
huge decision
without
me?

Dad

starts to say,

Willow, **why** *didn't you—*

I interrupt: *You* **can't** *blame it*

all on me, Dad. Then **they** give each other

that look, like all the adults **trust** each other

and none of them want to know **me**, I mean really

know me, who I really am, what I really think, why

I do what I do, or don't do what they think I should.

Dad starts to answer, looks at me, closes his mouth.

He doesn't want to fight about it any more than I do.

He waits for me to say more, but I don't, and neither

does he, and neither does Mom, for a long time.

Silence stalks around us like a cat. Even Zanna

doesn't chatter it into pieces. I look around

at these five people and at the beautiful

dog we love. I take a deep breath.

Will you listen to me? I ask.

Much to my surprise,

they do. *Let me tell*

you, I begin,

why I love

Roxy.

In
case you
haven't noticed,
I say, *I'm not exactly*
Miss Popularity. (They could
try to act surprised, but never mind.)
In fact, I only have one friend, and now
it looks like she likes a boy better than me,
so Roxy might be my best friend. I know that
may sound a little pathetic, but Roxy is always
glad to see me. I count on her. **I want** *to take care*
of her, and I know I might need **a little help**—*a lot*
of help—*from you guys. I know it's* **true** *that it's my*
fault she's blind, and maybe you think a **friend** *would*
not want to let someone suffer like this, but she could
get better! Maybe the vet is wrong; maybe Roxy won't
be blind forever. Even if she is blind, she's still Roxy.
It's probably the longest speech I have ever made.
I'm amazed: they all listen right to the end. They
actually seem to be thinking about what I said.
Zanna walks right up to Roxy and holds out
her hand for Roxy to sniff; Roxy licks
Zanna's hand, and Zanna pats her
on the head and grins. Then she
comes over to me, gives me
a long, serious look,
and says, *Willow,*
can I be your
friend,
too?

We

all say

what we love

about **Roxy**. Dad says,

*She always **seems to** know what I*

*expect, like she can **listen** to my thoughts.*

Mom says, *Roxy came **to us** when we were sad*

and brought her happiness to us. Grandma looks

at Mom like she's waiting for her to go on, but Mom

stops at that, and Grandma says, *Roxy has always been*

gentle with children. Zanna thinks about that, then says,

I'm not as scared of her as I used to be before, when she

could see. Grandpa listens to everyone, holding Roxy's

head in his lap, stroking her ears. *I've been thinking,*

he says. He looks at me. He looks at Mom and Dad.

Maybe it's time for us to tell Willow—he pauses

just a split second, like I do sometimes

when I'm not sure if I should say

something I want to say,

and then he finishes

the most amazing

sentence—*about*

the other

baby.

Diamond, Willow's twin sister (Roxy)

Last night, when I slept beside Willow, curled next to her in the shelter under the tree, I recalled when we were together long ago.

It was warm and dark. Something like a river pulsed through us and around us. We heard music. We heard voices. They were softer there than they are here. For a while, Willow and I moved together in a kind of dance—maybe it was then I learned to love to run, moving my arms and legs so freely. But we grew bigger; it became more difficult to move. Soon we could hardly move at all. It seemed the space closed in on us, tighter and tighter, until the day Willow left me there alone. I didn't know where she had gone—it seemed like she just disappeared.

And then I followed. For a while I didn't know where Willow was. I was in a room with bright lights, loud noises, people moving everywhere, handing me from one person to another, laying me down, picking me up, washing me and wrapping me in blankets.

Our parents held us in their arms and chose our names.

Look how long and thin she is, and so strong—she won't let go of my finger. They named my sister Willow.

This one is so beautiful. Look at her bright eyes—she looks like she can see right through you. We will call her Diamond.

It was only later that they gave both names to Willow.

We need to run a few more tests.

. . . twisted so she cannot eat or drink . . . inoperable . . . nothing we can do . . .

. . . four or five days if we keep her here . . . no more than two days if you take her home.

We will take both our babies home.

Three days in the hospital, one day and night at home. That's all I knew of being human.

An airplane ride, cradled in my father's arms, Willow in our mother's arms beside us.

Cool air against my face.

The smell of spruce trees.

An open door. A woodstove with a chair beside it. Grandma sitting in it, rocking. They put me in her arms. She looked at me and told a riddle: *I see a dewdrop shining at the center of a rose.*

Grandpa whispered, *You'll be back. I'll watch for you.*

Marty was six years old. He kissed my hair, and asked, *Why, Mommy? She looks perfect.* They let him hold me in his little arms, and he looked at me so deeply, I wondered later, when he held me as a puppy and looked at me that same way, if he might recognize me. I'm certain no one else does. Not even Grandpa.

That one night in their house, I slept beside Willow. They covered us with a soft yellow blanket and they all sat beside our crib. Our father played a long, slow song on his guitar. Our mother sang to us. Our brother reached into the crib and held our tiny hands. The room grew dark. Through a window, red and green and purple lights shimmered in the sky. A beautiful half moon shone on our faces.

I heard a wolf howl in the distance. Was it calling for me?

I loved the world and everything I saw and smelled and heard. I wanted more than anything to stay.

I went to sleep. Once I woke when Willow cried. Our mother picked her up and fed her, put her gently down.

She picked me up. She checked to see if I was breathing. She put her ear against my heart. It was still beating. She held me for a long time, then kissed me and put me back with Willow. I went to sleep.

In the morning, Willow woke, but I did not.

I
had
a sister,
a twin, not
identical. (They say,
She was so beautiful, as if that
proves the point.) *Why haven't you
told me this before?* I ask. Long silence,
before Mom answers, *I've always planned
to tell you. I know I've missed a few chances,
but it's hard to talk about her without crying,
and I don't like you to see me cry.* Dad says,
*We're so lucky to have you. I try not to think
too much about what might have been.*
Grandma looks at Grandpa, who says,
It was not our place to tell you.
Zanna says, *Don't blame me,
I didn't know.* Everyone
laughs at that. Roxy
gives a quick, sharp
bark, as if to say,
*Hey, I'm here,
too! I would
have told,
but who
listens
to a
dog?*

Why

are they

telling me this

today? When they

were worrying about me

last night, did it remind them

of those four nights Diamond was alive?

Or are they telling me that they know how it feels

to love someone you can't help, like I love Roxy now?

It's like walking through the kind of **deep** snow where each step

makes you break through the crust and sink **down** to your knees.

After they tell me about Baby Diamond, **I** say, *Whatever we*

*decide about Roxy, I'll always **remember** the day we all*

*went to pick her out. Remember **her** intelligent*

clear eyes? (Will we ever see them again?)

I say *Whatever we decide,* like it's

obvious to everyone: no matter

what happens, I'm part of it

as much as they are.

Dad nods, *Yes,*

he says, *I do*

remember

Roxy's

eyes

that

day.

Roxy (Diamond)

I like hearing Willow say she remembers my eyes from the day they brought me home. I remember her eyes that day, too.

I was born to a malamute who had led her team through six Iditarods, winning one of them. We were so proud of that. All the puppies scrambled for attention, tumbling over each other to get our mother to notice us. Maybe we'd grow up to win races like she did.

But there were too many of us in that dog yard. The musher put out word that she was selling puppies, and people started coming by. They'd look us over, ask a lot of questions, and sometimes leave with one of us. I figured out that if I tucked my head into my paws, closed my eyes, and pretended to sleep until they left, no one would notice me.

So I was "sleeping" when I heard voices I remembered from way back in another life. I opened one eye and saw a big boy, a little girl, and a man and woman I thought I'd seen before. The woman was wearing a red jacket that she could barely close.

I opened both eyes and watched them closely.

Willow, look at this one, said the man. The whole family came and looked me over. I stared at Willow and she stared at me—a long, deep gaze. She got down on her knees and held me in her lap. I licked her face, and she looked up, eyes shining.

Let's take her home, Dad! Willow said.

They brought me home and put fresh straw in my doghouse. They fed me well, and I was happy.

Until the day they came home with the baby. When they took her inside their house, I wanted so much to go in with them, I started howling. I couldn't stop for hours. Willow and Marty came out, bringing extra food and water. I ate and drank, and then I howled some more.

Roxy, what's wrong? they kept asking. But of course I couldn't tell them.

I couldn't say, *I want to be the baby, not that one you call Suzanna.*

That's when Marty looked at me, that penetrating look that made me wonder if he knew me. All he said was, *Maybe she's jealous of the baby.*

Willow answered, *Why—just because Mom and Dad sit around looking at her whenever they aren't feeding her, talking about her, or giving her a bath?*

Marty laughed. *Come on,* he said, *let's hitch up Cora and I'll take you for a ride in my new sled. Get away from Babyland for a while.*

I watched them, wishing I could ride in the sled with Willow, knowing my best hope was that maybe someday I could grow up and pull the sled with Cora.

Once

we start

talking—really

talking—it doesn't take

us long to decide to keep Roxy.

Mom canceled the vet appointment

when she saw I'd taken off. She said she

and Dad were relieved that Roxy was alive—

even while we were sick with worry about you.

So maybe in a way I did help, just not the way I

planned it. **We all** agree that Roxy should go home

with us. I **get** her settled into Dad's sled, hitched to

the snowmachine. ***What** about me?* Zanna asks, and

Dad hugs her and says, ***We want** you to go with*

Willow, in her sled, Zanna. She thinks about it,

then stands up tall and says, *Okay, I'll help*

my sister. So Mom rides with Roxy,

and I take all five dogs and Zanna.

We head home together and we

stay together on the trail.

We arrive without

any trouble.

Not one

bit.

When
Marty heard that
I was missing, he flew
home to help look for me.
By the time he got here, we
were all back, but he's staying
an extra day anyway, and Mom
is letting me miss a day of school
to be with him. He stares at Roxy
like she's made of gold, then looks
at me like I'm his equal. *Hey*—he
puts his hand on my head—*I think
you're taller, Willow.* I smile. *No,*
I say, *I'm not; you must be shorter.*
He laughs. **Marty always** does this:
laughs like he **is** really enjoying me,
but with a look **on** his face like he
understands that **my** joking has
a serious **side**, and there's
more to me than
most people
see.

I
ask
Marty
why he's never
told me about Diamond.
You were Zanna's age when we
were born—I know you must remember.
(It's weird to say that: *we were born.*) Marty
answers, *How do little kids learn all the things*
they're not supposed to talk about? Poop and farts
and sex, Uncle Henry's drinking, Mom's gray hair. He
turns to **look at** me . . . *And the other baby, those few days*
she lived, ***the*** *birchbark box of Diamond's ashes, scattered*
in a secret, ***sacred*** *place. You were with us,* he tells me.
In my ***memory****, you're wide awake. Mom is carrying*
you, zipped up inside that red down jacket she wore
when she was pregnant. I know the one he means;
she wore it before Zanna was born; she still
has it. *Where?* I ask him. *Where is the*
secret, sacred place? Marty says,
Come on, let's hitch up Lucky,
Cora, Samson, and Magoo.
I still know the way.
I'll take you
there.

I

love

riding

in the sled with

Marty driving. New

snow looks like diamonds . . .

like ashes . . . like Diamond's ashes . . .

I'm daydreaming, looking around, so I don't

notice when Marty turns the dogs onto the old trail,

the one Kaylie and I took by mistake when we got lost.

When Marty stops the dogs, I look around. Could he know

this is the exact spot where Kaylie and I camped out that night?

Or could it be that maybe **Cora remembers** when we stopped here,

and that's why she stops now? But Marty says, *This is the place.* He looks

around like he's in church. *This is the **place** they scattered Diamond's ashes.*

Marty couldn't have heard **from** Mom and Dad that this is where Kaylie and I

camped. I haven't told them. ***Way back then***, Marty says, *the spruce tree was*

much smaller. When they spread the ashes on its branches, it reminded me

of falling snow. I blink. *It was snow,* I say, *that kept us warm that night.*

Marty looks at me. *What night?* he asks. I tell him about camping

here, and staying warm under the snowy branches of this tree.

We see a spruce hen sitting on one of the low branches.

Is it the same one I saw that night? It looks

at me and doesn't fly away. I say,

Hi. Don't I know you from

somewhere? I almost

hear it answer, *Hello*

Willow. Yes, my

dear, you

do.

My
diamond
willow stick
is almost finished. I'm
sanding each diamond one last time
before I polish it, trying to figure out why
Kaylie has so many friends and I don't. Could it be
because she's happy all the time? **Maybe.** That would be
kind of interesting, if **being happy** gets you friends and
having friends **makes you happy.** I don't want
a million friends, just enough so that
if one friend starts eating lunch
with a boy, I don't have to
sit there all by myself.
Tomorrow, I'll go
back to school.
I wish I felt
happier
about
that.

Dad
and I go with
Marty to the airport
and watch his plane take off.
On the way home, I tell Dad about
the coincidence, how Marty showed me
their sacred place, and it was the same place I
camped that night. Dad nods, then asks, *Do you know*
why we picked that place to scatter Baby Diamond's ashes?
(Of course I don't. I was six days old; no one ever told me.)
That was where I found the diamond willow stick—the one
you're working on. So in a way, that place is where your
name came from—your names. **I'm not** sure how I feel
about them giving me **both** names. I ask Dad, *Why*
*does diamond **willow** have the diamond shapes?*
He thinks for a minute **and** answers, *As I*
*understand it, a **diamond** forms*
in the sapwood at a place
of injury, or sickness,
a place where a
branch has
fallen
away.

Cora (Willow's great-grandfather's sister)

It looks like Roxy got herself back into the house, where she's always wanted to be. I should try something like that, break a leg or something, see if they'll take me inside, too. Sit by the fire like I used to, before they got the idea to hitch me up. Whose crazy idea was that, anyway, to take a mutt like me and try to make a sled dog out of me? Oh well, I did my best. I was a good leader when I was young, and I can still do it when I have to.

I understand all their commands, and I usually follow them. They like that. But I've lived around here for a long, long time, and I know a thing or two. So sometimes I take them places they should go, even if it's not what they're telling me. A few days before the twin babies were born, I brought their father to the diamond willow grove. I knew how much he loved that beautiful, light-dark diamond willow wood. It makes a good strong stick you can hold on to when you're walking up a long hill in the dark.

Less than a week later, I brought the family back. One baby was wrapped inside her mother's jacket (that was Willow) and the other—well, I knew what had happened. They were all so deep in their grief, I'm not sure they could have found the place again, but I know that old trail well, and I took them right to it. Marty had two different colored mittens, brown and green—I remember that because the green one kept falling off, and I'd pick it up in my mouth and bring it to him.

That tree wasn't much taller than he was at the time.

For a few years, I took them all out there every year on Diamond's birthday. But it was Willow's birthday, too, and I suppose they wanted her to have happy birthdays like other children, so they stopped doing that. The night I took Willow and Kaylie out there was the first time in years I'd been back there myself.

The storm came in fast that afternoon. The girls are young; they didn't know how ferocious it would be. I knew they'd need a place to sleep that night, and I was pretty sure I had less than an hour to get them to a place they might find shelter. So I headed down the old trail to see if I could find the diamond willow grove. The trail was over-grown; no one uses it much these days.

I might have missed the place altogether if that spruce hen hadn't flown along with us. When I saw her stop to rest on a low branch of the spruce tree, I stopped to look around, and sure enough, I recognized the place I remember from so long ago.

Roxy was in the sled; her eyes were bandaged, but she acted like she knew where we were. How? I've never figured out who Roxy was in her human life—no one I remember knowing. All I can say is, she was more content than I've ever seen her, curled up with Willow through that long dark night as the blizzard raged and then subsided.

I

want

to tell Kaylie

about everything I've

learned since I last saw her.

(It's only been two days, but it

seems like two years.) I get to the

lunchroom first and find an empty table.

While I'm waiting for Kaylie, Richard sees

me and starts to come toward my table. *No!*

I almost shout, but I manage not to say a word.

I just look away, thinking, *I can't talk to Kaylie*

if he's here. Even though I don't say anything,

he swerves away at the last minute, and sits by

himself at the next table. Kaylie comes in and

sees us both. She hesitates, like she isn't sure

which table to sit at. **What** should I do?

I think fast. I know **if I do** nothing, my

best friend will **have a** hard choice

to make. My **Diamond** story can

wait. For once, **inside** myself,

I don't start a big argument.

I get up and move over

to Richard's table.

Kaylie smiles

and joins

us.

In
about
two minutes
our table is full
and someone pushes
another table up next to it
so there are nine kids sitting here.
That's not surprising. Everyone likes
Kaylie and Richard. But here's the surprise:
Almost every **other** time I've been with these kids,
the group I call the sparkly **people**, I've tried really hard
to make myself invisible. Now they **are** all asking questions
about our night out in the storm, and I'm **kind of** enjoying myself.
It's partly because I'm thinking up some **interesting** answers but also
because I start wondering what makes people ask the things they ask.
Why does Amber want to know if I was more scared of the dark
or the cold? What makes Nicholas so curious about the
lynx: *What did it sound like? How big were the*
tracks? Did you smell anything when it
got close to you? Richard's friend
Jon asks me, *How's Roxy?*
Will she ever see again?
I can't answer. Without
warning, my eyes
flood with tears.
Jon is quiet.
I bet she
will, he
says.

Roxy
lies on my bed
with her head resting
on her paws, like she thinks
she has always belonged here.
When I **come home** from school, I
call out to her—*Hey, **Roxy***—and she perks
up her ears, moves over to make room for me,
tilts her head to one side as if she's asking what's
happened while I've been gone all day. I talk to her
for so long, I almost forget to check her eyes. I've
promised Mom and Dad I'll do that every day.
Today, for the first time, her eyes seem to be
a little better, not so crusty. I wash them
with warm water, dry them. She keeps
them closed while I put on a fresh
bandage. I get my Dinak'i book
and work on my homework
and Roxy sits with me,
her head in my lap,
so peaceful, so
right.

Roxy (Diamond)

After Willow washes my eyes, she leaves the room to get a clean bandage, and I open my eyes for a minute, first both at once, then one at a time. I see light through a window. I see a shadow in the doorway. The shadow moves away so fast, I know it must be Zanna. She says she isn't scared of me anymore, but she still steers clear of me when we're alone.

No one knows that I used to snap and growl at Zanna. She was so small, barely walking; she'd come close and reach out her hand to pet me like Marty and Willow did.

I wanted to be a baby, and get bigger, and learn to walk. I wanted them to take me inside when I got cold, like they took Zanna in whenever she let out the smallest squawk.

And so, when she came close, I'd growl at her, low in my throat, so no one else could hear.

Once I nipped at Zanna's ankle and she started crying. Willow called her a crybaby: *Oh, Zanna,* she said, *you know Roxy wouldn't hurt you.* Zanna looked at Willow, then back at me, like she didn't know whether to believe her sister or herself. After that, she never came near me again.

It was a long time ago. I'd never do that now. Zanna might not even remember why she's scared of me.

Did
I see Roxy
open her left eye and
close it again? Zanna says
Roxy winked at her last night.
I don't believe her, of course—
only a little kid would believe
that a dog **can** wink—but I
wonder if **Roxy** is getting
better. I **see** her pulling
at her bandage with
her paw when
she doesn't
know I'm
looking.

If
you
can see,
open one eye,
I whisper in Roxy's
left ear. I know she hears me,
but I don't think she understands.
I've taken off her bandage. Her eyes
look better, but she keeps them closed.
Roxy, do you want to go for a sled ride?
When she hears that, she jumps off the
bed as if to say, *When **are** we leaving?*
I say, *Look over **there**, Roxy!* I point
first one way, then a **different** way,
to see if she looks the **ways** I point,
but Roxy will have none **of** that.
Either she isn't **seeing** much
or she is refusing to let me
know that she can see.
Okay, Roxy, I'll
take you out
for a ride.
Let's
go.

Roxy

and Cora

jump around like

little kids, licking each other

and rolling in the snow together.

I hitch up all the dogs, with Cora as the

leader. Then I try to get **Roxy** into the sled, but

she acts like she **doesn't want to** go after all.

*I thought you wanted a sled **ride**,* I say.

Come on, cooperate with me. Her

eyes are closed. It's not

like Roxy to be

so difficult.

I turn

away from her

for about half a minute; when

I turn back and look at her, **she** is holding

a harness in her mouth, like she **wants to** tell

me something. Did Roxy **pull** the harness out of

my emergency kit? How could she do that

if she can't see? What is going on here?

Roxy, look at me, I say, and she does!

For a split second, Roxy blinks

her eyes—open, shut—that

clear pure brown,

shining like

the sun

itself.

I
pull
the harness
gently over Roxy's
ears, very carefully over her
closed eyes. I whisper to her, *If you*
think you can do this, **Roxy***, I'll let you try.*
How should I hitch her? She **and Cora** work well
together. I'll let them both lead. They **are so** excited,
and I know that Prince and Lucky are **smart** enough
to follow my commands, no matter who is leading.
I give all the dogs a pep talk: *You know the trails.*
We'll take it slow this first time, see how it goes.
I haven't told anyone I think Roxy can see
a little bit. I'm not sure why. I just
have a feeling it's something
she wants to keep
secret.

I

can

think better

out here with my dogs,

the sound of the sled runners,

quiet as my thoughts, inside me

and around me, all at the same time.

It's so amazing that **Roxy is** keeping up

with Cora! Is she **telling me** that she can

see? Or is she saying **something** else, like:

*Seeing isn't as **important** as you think.*

Roxy is such a pretty dog, so smart.

Everyone always loves her,

but none of us knew

how tough she

could

be.

It's
hard to say
who's leading.
Roxy and Cora and I
all seem to have the same idea
of where we're going. The dogs turn
off onto the old trail before I tell them to.
When we arrive at the diamond willow grove,
they both come to a stop before **I can** even say *Whoa.*
I want to know if Roxy is going to **keep** her eyes closed here.
When I look, they are wide open, like **a secret** passageway between
her thoughts and my own. *Roxy,* I am thinking to her, *did you know
I had a sister? Her name was Diamond and she died, just four days
after she was born. They brought her ashes here because of these
diamond willow trees. This is where they got our name.* Roxy
thinks back to me, *Oh yes, Willow. I know about Diamond.
I know her as well as I know you.* For some reason, I
am not surprised. Then Roxy thinks, *Willow,
don't tell anyone that I can see.*
I understand that, too. Now
we're both thinking
together, *This
will be our
secret.*
Yes.

Cora (Willow's great-grandfather's sister)

When Willow looks into Roxy's eyes, I can hear them thinking to each other. The other dogs don't listen, so I'm the only witness. I don't think they know that I can hear.

I figured out who Roxy must have been when she was human. She was the baby they called Diamond.

I remember Diamond shining like a star in that brief time that she was here. Everyone kept saying she was perfect. Well, of course she was perfect: she didn't live long enough to do anything wrong.

No one would say the same for Roxy—when she was a puppy, she was always causing trouble. Once she chewed a hole in the screen door and tried to push herself through. She got her head stuck and pulled it back out; then she gave up and went to sleep under the aspen tree. When everyone came home, Roxy looked so innocent, they looked around to see who could have done it, and guess who took the blame? I got blamed for lots of things that Roxy did. It never bothered me too much. I liked Roxy just as much as they did.

Come to think of it, Roxy was always trying to get into the house. There was that time when she was a little bigger, and she started digging under the front door. When the hinges loosened and the door swung open, Roxy ran inside. I heard them say they found her hiding under some clothes in a corner of Willow's closet. They put her back out in the dog yard with the rest of us, and for days she drove us crazy with her howling. No one, including me, could figure out what was wrong.

Now I think I understand—if Roxy is Willow's twin, of course she wants to stay inside.

At

last,

Kaylie and I

have a chance to be

alone. Mom is taking Zanna

to the dentist, Dad is working late, and

Richard has basketball practice after school.

Kaylie meets me at my locker and we walk to my

house together. First she tells me every detail of every

conversation she and Richard have had in the past week.

Then finally she asks: *How are you, Willow? How is Roxy?*

(It feels like all one question.) When **I tell** her what I found out

about having a twin sister (I love this about **Kaylie**), she stops

in her tracks to stare at me, like she **almost** doesn't believe me,

but she does. So I tell her **everything** I know about Diamond.

Remember where we found shelter the night of the blizzard?

She remembers. *Well,* I say, *It's almost like that's the place*

where Diamond lives. I tell her how Roxy and Cora took

the sled there, and she asks, *Are Roxy's eyes healed?*

I think, *Yes!* But I'm careful. I say, *Maybe, almost.*

Kaylie asks, *I mean, can Roxy see?* I hesitate.

I half answer, *How would I know that?*

I hate to do that to my best friend,

but—I'm pretty sure of this—

I made a promise to my

other best friend,

Roxy.

Roxy

sleeps

curled up

on my bed, and

I dream of Diamond

here beside me. **We** are both

the age I am now. In the **dream**, we're

at school and we're sitting at **the same** table.

I'm thinking, *This must be a **dream**,* because all

the sparkly kids who always sit **together** are asking

if they can sit with us. They're all coming up to us and

saying *Diamond, Willow, can we sit here?* (Or are they

saying *Diamond Willow*?) I'm quiet, like I always am,

while Diamond is saying, *Sure, just save that place*

for Kaylie, and, *Good luck in the game tonight,*

and, *Are you coming to our party tomorrow?*

Our party? I forgot—tomorrow is my (our)

birthday. I've never had a party. (I'm not

sure I'd know how.) I wake up, but I

don't open my eyes because I know

Diamond will be gone when I do.

After a while, I open one eye—

and there's Roxy, sitting

right where I've been

looking, in the

dream, at

Diamond.

Dad
and Mom,
with Kaylie's help,
planned a surprise party—*For*
you and Roxy, Kaylie says, *because*
Roxy's almost better, and you're thirteen.
Marty's home; Grandma and Grandpa came;
Zanna got to invite one of her friends, and Kaylie
invited four kids we know from school (Richard,
two quiet kids that Kaylie and I both like, and that
boy called Jon—he's been saying he wants to meet
Roxy). Usually I'd hate this kind of surprise. More
than seven people in a room, and **I'm** off hiding in a
closet somewhere. Thirteen, I'm **actually** sweating,
if not crying. But Roxy is **enjoying** all the attention
everyone is showering on her. ***This** dog,* Richard
announces, *was nearly blinded, and could have*
died when she was out all night in the worst
blizzard of the year—yet look at her now!
Let's have a toast to Roxy! Okay, he's
been watching a little too much TV,
but we do look at Roxy: her eyes
are closed, and she's grinning
the way dogs do, that look
that says, *If only I could*
talk, I'd have a few
things to tell
you.

I'm

not sure

how the kids

will react when

Grandma starts telling

riddles. *I see something,* she says.

Someone is untangling his dog lines.

Pretty soon those dogs will start howling.

I laugh, because I know **this is** Grandma's

way to have some gentle **fun**, teasing Dad.

Jon looks all around the room and guesses:

I think I might know the answer. Maybe

it's your father, changing the strings

on his guitar. Pretty good, for his

first time meeting Grandma.

He glances over at me

like he's hoping

I'm impressed

and that I'll

smile, and

I am

and

do.

I'm
almost finished
sanding and polishing my
diamond willow stick. Dad sits down
with me and asks what I want to use it for.
He shows me a picture of a diamond willow lamp.
I love that idea! Dad helps me measure and plan it, and
then he starts talking about **Roxy**. *Do you think she's well
enough to go back outside? It **makes** sense to move her back
before she gets used to being indoors.* **Me**? Dad is asking me
what I think about Roxy? No one is going to **laugh** at what I
have to say, or pretend to listen and then ignore me? I say,
Roxy should stay inside. Dad doesn't argue, but he seems
a little doubtful. And then, as if someone planned this,
just at that moment, a mouse runs across the room.
Squeak, squeak! it says, and Roxy goes, *Arf, Arf!*
and the mouse runs back into its little hole,
and Dad says, *Come to think of it, that's
the first mouse I've seen in here since
Roxy's been inside.* So just like that
it's all settled: Roxy is our new
mouser. I go over to her and
stroke her ears, smiling.
No one else is looking,
so Roxy opens both
her eyes and
laughs.

A
perfect
trail, a perfect
day: new snow—quiet,
dry, and sparkling, the kind
that doesn't hurt the dogs' feet.
The days are getting longer, warmer,
twenty above zero instead of twenty below.
I'm running all six dogs, with Cora and Roxy
leading the team like two wings of a swan.
I feel like **I am** flying with them, like my
twin sister **Diamond** is alive inside me
saying, ***Willow**, this is happiness.*
Me, these dogs, this snow, the
spruce hen flying just
ahead of us: *This is
happiness.* I
see.

Jean, Willow's great-great-great grandmother (Spruce Hen)

Almost every day now, Willow is out here with her dogs. Up and down the old trails and the new ones. She knows her way around about as well as I do.

Sometimes Willow gives someone a ride—Zanna, or Kaylie and Richard, or Jon.

It's not so dark now, these late afternoons when she comes home and melts snow for the dogs.

Today, after all the dogs are fed and watered, Willow turns to Roxy: *Come on, let's go inside.*

Later, when the sun goes down, a light comes on in Willow's room, shining from the lamp that Willow and her father made. In the circle of its light, Willow sits cross-legged on the bed with Roxy.

It looks for all the world like the two of them are deep in conversation.

ACKNOWLEDGMENTS

I thank—

Everyone at Farrar, Straus and Giroux for all they do. Special thanks to Frances Foster for her vision, wisdom, and friendship, and to Janine O'Malley for her countless manifestations of thoughtful support.

The people of Telida, Nikolai, and McGrath, Alaska; special thanks to Agnes Eluska Marker, who read the manuscript and answered my questions.

Dr. Eliza Jones, Athabascan elder, scholar, and trusted friend, for careful reading and thoughtful suggestions.

Jeff King, Iditarod champion, for help with dog-mushing questions; Louise Magoon for medical knowledge; Bob Gander and Ken Laninga for information about diamond willow.

Good readers Danae DeJournett; Mary Clare DuRocher; Ana, Cara, and Gretchen Liuzzi; Ingrid Wendt; Claire Ewart; and members of the Indiana Society of Children's Book Writers and Illustrators.

My family and the animals who live with us and around us. Special love and thanks to the Bartlett family; to Glen; and to Lloyd, Penny, Cameron, and Jordan, and their dog, Roxanne. As always, thanks to Chad—and a quick smile to the mouse who ran through our house and blinked at us.

HELEN FROST
Answers Questions from Her Readers

Have you ever ridden a dog sled? Did you go very fast? Have you ever crashed?
Yes, I've ridden several dog sleds, not too fast. I've never crashed. My experience in crashing has been on bikes, cross-country skis, and one time running down a sand dune, knowing I was going too fast and about to lose my balance, and then I did. The worst part was that my father had a movie camera going, and recorded my face-down-splat-in-the-sand for everyone to watch over and over again.

Why were you in Alaska?
My aunt lived in Alaska when I was a child. When she came to visit, she showed slides and told stories about living there; that was when I first wanted to go to Alaska.

Later, I became a teacher and taught for three years in a one-teacher school in Telida, a small (25 people) Athabascan community in the interior part of the state. The people who lived there became like family to me.

At other times, I worked at Denali National Park, raised small children in Fairbanks, and taught fifth grade in Ketchikan.

Do you follow the Iditarod?
When I lived in Telida, the Iditarod came through the nearby towns of Nikolai, McGrath, and Takotna, so I followed it closely during those years. One year, one of the mushers, Miki Collins, was from a town near Telida, and the whole school went to Nikolai to cheer her on (remember this was a small school, nine students that year). Miki later mentioned us in a book she wrote, *Trapline Twins*, describing how we met her and gave her grape juice when she arrived in Nikolai after midnight.

I've known several other mushers, too—I met Herbie Nayokpuk in Shishmaref before I knew anything about the Iditarod, and later found out that he was very well-known and much loved by Iditarod mushers and fans. I met Jeff King just as he was beginning his racing career, and now he's won the Iditarod four times. When I was writing *Diamond Willow*, Jeff read the manuscript and answered my questions about sled dogs.

How many times do you have to rewrite a poem to get it to fit in your shape?
It used to be possible to answer this question. When I wrote poems mostly on paper, I could just count the number of different pages, and that would be how many times I rewrote the poem. For *Diamond Willow*, I wrote each poem in a rough shape on paper, and then worked on the computer to finish it. The changes were ongoing, so I can't count the drafts. I can only answer "lots."

Do you ever get sick of following your own rules when you write poems?
When it's working, as it did in this final form of *Diamond Willow*, it's fun, and I don't get sick of it. But sometimes before I find the form for a new book, I work with my own rules for several months before admitting to myself that it's not working. That's not fun. If it happens, I take a break and then come back and try something new. When I eventually do find the form that moves the story forward, it's exciting to see it all fall into place.

Have you ever met Gary Paulsen?
I've met him the way you've met me—by reading his books. Once I heard him speak, but I didn't have a chance to talk with him personally.

How cold does it get in Alaska?
Alaskans like to say things like, "It's so cold that you can spit and hear it crackle before it hits the ground." But when it really is that cold (40–60 degrees below zero), you're too busy keeping a birch fire going in the woodstove, and trying to keep your boot liners dry, and cooking big pots of moose soup, to ever remember to spit in order to find out if that saying is true.

One thing I love is on a day when it gets warmer after it has been cold for a long time, there are patches of warmer air, like someone is stirring the air, and you can walk from bitter cold into a warmer place. It might still be very cold—maybe 20 below instead of 40 below—but you can feel the difference as you walk along.

Another thing I love is the Northern Lights.

Did you know that you can hear things from farther away on a cold day?

DISCUSSION QUESTIONS

Note: None of these questions has a "right answer." They are suggestions of things you might think about or talk over with someone else who has read *Diamond Willow*.

1. Do you think Willow is lonely? Is being lonely the same as being alone?

2. Is having a pet just as good as having a person-friend?

3. What does Willow discover that makes it easier for her to make new friends?

4. Have you ever experienced the death of someone who loves you? If so, do you sometimes feel like their love for you is still somewhere in the world, as expressed by the animals in *Diamond Willow*?

WRITING IDEAS

1. Try writing a diamond-shaped poem of your own. Can you put a "hidden message" inside it?

2. Observe an animal without writing anything down. Pay close attention to what sounds it makes, how it moves, what it eats, how it relates to other animals, and how it relates to people. Then write a story or poem from the point of view of the animal. Give it to someone to read, without naming the animal, and see if they can figure out "who" is speaking.?

3. Make your own rules for a poem and see how hard it is to follow them. If it doesn't lead you to discover something fun or interesting, try a different rule.

    Examples:
    • A poem of three stanzas, four lines each, that has a different color in each stanza.
    • A poem shaped like a circle, square, triangle, or rectangle.
    • A poem, at least ten lines long, that doesn't say anything true.

THINGS YOU MIGHT LIKE

Spinning Through the Universe **by Helen Frost**
If you enjoy trying to write in the voices of different people, or using different forms (rules) for your poems, this book will give you a lot of new ideas.

Websites

http://iditarodblogs.com/zuma
Zuma's Paw Prints, using the Iditarod in the classroom

www.iditarod.com
the official Iditarod website

www.helenfrost.net
Helen Frost's website

An accidental kidnapping leaves unanswered questions.

Years later, the truth is revealed.

A NOVEL BY PRINTZ HONOR BOOK AUTHOR

HELEN FROST

Keep reading for an excerpt from

HIDDEN

by Helen Frost

1

I was a happy little girl wearing a pink dress,
    sitting in our gold minivan,
    dancing with my doll, Kamara.

       I'll be right back, Mom promised.
       Leave the music on, I begged,
           so she left her keys
           dangling
      while she
          ran in to pay for gas
          and buy a Diet Coke.

2

I think about that little girl
    the way you might remember your best friend
        who moved away.
    Sitting in the middle seat
      beside an open window,
      her seatbelt fastened,
      she looked out at the world.

3

And then she heard
    a gunshot
    from inside the store.

That's when she—when I—
    stopped breathing.
        I clicked my seatbelt off,
        dived into the back, and
        ducked down on the floor
            to hide
                under a blanket
            · until Mom
                came back out.

I heard the car door open, heard it close.
    The music stopped.
    Why? Mom liked that song.

I breathed again. (Mom smelled like cigarettes.)

I pushed the blanket off my face,
    opened my mouth
    to ask,
        What happened in there?

But then I heard a word Mom wouldn't say.
    A man's voice.
    C'mon! Start! He was yelling at our car—
        ˏ and the car
            obeyed him.

It started up
    just like it thought
        Mom was driving.

4

Who *was* driving?
Had this man just shot someone? Had he
    shot . . . Mom?
If he found out I was back there
    what would he do to me?
    I pulled the blanket back over my face.
        (Pretend you're Kamara.
        Don't breathe. Don't move.
        Be as small as you can—smaller.)

Sand on the floor of the car. I pressed hard.
    It stuck to my skin.
    I pressed harder.
        (Breathe
        if you have to,
        but don't move a muscle.)

Like a small rabbit
    that knows a cat is close by,
    I paid attention. I didn't
                            twitch.

5

I could tell which way we were headed—
    we stopped at the King Street stoplight.
        Left turn . . . right turn . . . left . . .

He sped up.
Was he trying to throw the police off our trail?

He stopped, got out of the car.
Where were we?
He got back in,
                    drove off faster.

Sirens?
        Yes—coming closer!

One time in first grade,
        a police officer came to our class.
                "If someone tries to grab you," she said,
                "wave your arms, kick your legs.
                Yell at the top of your lungs,
                THIS MAN IS NOT MY FATHER."

The sirens meant
        someone might stop us—
                I could jump up.
                I could wave.
                I could yell.

But it didn't happen.
We drove faster, farther.
        The sirens
                faded away in the distance.

Long straight road . . . curvy road . . .

Fast for a while. No stops.
　　Right turn.
　　Left turn.
　　　　Stop. Go. Turn . . .
　　　　I swallowed the panic that rose.
　　　　　　I didn't throw up.

6

Sound of gravel. Dust in my throat.
(Don't cough!)
Bumping along that dusty road,
　　screaming inside.
　　(Dad, where are you? Mom?)
　　　　A phone rang—Dad's ring on Mom's phone!
　　　　Mom must have left her phone in the car.
　　　　　　Her whole purse, down on the floor?

　　(Do not—do not!—jump up and grab it.)
　　I clenched my hands together.

GPS, the man snarled—I heard him dump
　　　　Mom's purse upside down.
　　　　He opened a window.
　　　　He closed it.

(Did he just toss Mom's phone out the window?)

7

I put my thumb in my mouth
　　like a little baby. I pulled my knees
　　　　to my chin, and closed my eyes tight.

Where were we going?
What would happen to me when we got there?

After a long time—
　　it felt like hours—
　　　　the car slowed down.
　　We made a sharp turn.
We stopped.
He got out.
I heard a garage door open.
He got back in the car.
　　Forward.
　　Stop.
　　The garage door came down.
　　　　The car door opened, slammed shut.
　　I heard a dog.
　　　　Barking or growling?
　　　In the garage or outside?
Another door opened
　　　　and closed.
　　　　Had the man gone somewhere?

8

Carefully, I pushed back the blanket
　　and looked around.

I was alone
in a very dark place.

I might have been wrong about Mom's phone.
I kept my head low,
climbed into the middle seat,
leaned far enough forward
so I could see into the front.
Mom's water bottle—not quite empty.
A chocolate chip granola bar.
Kleenex.
ChapStick.
Checkbook.
Calendar.
Her little album of pictures—
me and Alex, her and Dad.

No wallet—she took that into the store.
No phone.

9
Where was I?
A messy garage—rakes and shovels,
gas cans and broken-down boxes.

In the garage door,
higher than I could reach,
three small windows,
a few rays of sun shining through them.

Behind an old freezer—
a door—to outside?

A red-and-white boat
on a trailer
right next to the car.

If I could get out fast enough, he'd never know I was there.
I told myself what to do, and I did it:
Quietly—get out of the car with Kamara.
Take the granola bar. Leave the water—
if I take that, he might notice it's gone.
Carefully tiptoe across the floor.
(The dog—outside—still growl-barking.)
Squeeze behind the freezer.
Try to open the side door.

Locked
with a padlock
the size of my fist.

10

The freezer was empty, unplugged—it wouldn't be cold.
Could I get inside, and hide there?
No. A boy on the news
got stuck inside an old freezer—
he suffocated to death
before his mom found him.
I shivered.

The boat?
    I might be tall enough
        to climb in
        if I stepped up on the trailer.

But I didn't dare move.

11

I don't know how long
    I stood there
    in my pink dress,
    mostly hidden
    behind the freezer.

12

A light came on. A door opened.
    I stopped breathing.

From another room, I heard
    happy voices—
        real people or on a TV?
        It was a TV—this was someone's house.

The man came out,
    opened the car door, closed it,
    went back inside.
    I was pretty sure
        he didn't look
            over at me.

13

I had to do something.
I ran to the boat
    and climbed in.
It was full of fishing stuff:
    nets and ropes
    a tackle box
    fishing poles
    a rusty coffee can.

    A blue cloth, partly stretched
        over the boat—
        could I hide under that?

At the boat's pointed end, a triangular place,
    like a little cave—I just fit.

A gray rag?
No—an old sweatshirt
    wadded up on the floor of the boat.
    I put it on—it covered my dress.
Yes,
    I could hide in the boat
    for a while.

14

I was hungry. Mom always said,
    Eat something, Wren. It helps you think.
        I unwrapped the granola bar, took one bite.
        One more. Another.
I tried to think.

Could I open the garage door?
If it was something to lift—could I lift it?
What if you had to know certain numbers to push?

If the door opened, he'd hear me.

Sooner or later, he'd leave the house. He had to.
Did anyone live there with him?

The dog barked louder.
It was outside, but not far away.
Had anyone fed it?

Through the windows in the garage door,
the sky
got darker and darker.

15

Someone turned on a light
and opened the door from the house.

I thought I heard something out here.
(A girl's voice?)

I didn't move, curled up in the boat,
clutching Kamara so hard
I thought she might break.

The man again, from inside:
Shut that door! Stay out of there!
You heard me—I SAID—

The light went off. The door slammed shut.
It sounded like somebody banged up against it.
　　　The girl yelled, *Ow! Quit it! That hurt!*
Then it got quiet.
After that,
　　　for a long time,
　　　nothing happened.

16

The garage door went up.
The light came on.
　　　Somewhere outside, a car door opened and closed.
I heard someone
　　　walk through the garage
　　　and open the door to the house.

A woman's voice: *What's this car doing here?*
The man: *How many times do I have to tell you—*
　　　　　stay out of my business.
The woman: *You keep a stolen car in our garage,*
　　　　　it's my business.

The light went off.
The garage door closed.
The other door slammed.
I heard shouting inside the house.
I couldn't hear words,
　　　but the man's voice was loud
　　　　　and mean.

17

I was shaking.
    Trying hard not to cry.
How could I sleep
    in the crowded boat?
I was thirsty.
Hungry.
I had to pee.

18

The light came on. The door from the house flew open.
    The woman: *This is the car they're searching for!*
        What happened
        to Wren Abbott?

    A voice on TV: *Once again,*
        the child is eight years old.
        Last seen wearing a pink dress,
        with matching beads in her hair.
        She may be holding a doll
        she calls Kamara.
        If you have any information
            please call—

19

The TV cut off.
The man: *Nothing to do with me!*
    You think I'm some kind of pervert,
    taking a little kid?

(What's a pervert?)

The woman: *Of course not. But, West,*
  did you check the backseat
  when you got in the car?

(The man's name is West.)

West: *No! There wasn't time!*
  None of this worked like we planned, Stacey.
  No one was going to get shot.

(*Who* got shot?)
(The woman is Stacey.)

I heard the car doors—opening, closing.

Stacey: *She's not in the car.*
  Where is she?

West: *Maybe she got out when I stopped*
  in the parking lot—I took a few minutes
  to take the plate off another car
  and put it on this one.

(That time he stopped—could I have jumped out?)

Stacey: *If she was lost in a parking lot,*
  someone would have found her by now.
  They've been searching for more than six hours!

West: *They can keep searching.*
Tomorrow, we paint the car.
We ditch it.
Nothing to pin on me.

Stacey: *West—this girl is Darra's age!*
We can call from a pay phone—anonymously—
tell them Wren Abbott is not in the car they're searching for.
At least we know that much!

(The girl is Darra.)

West: *We know NOTHING. You hear me?*
Stacey: *Let go of me!*

I'd never heard
the sound of one person hitting another,
but I knew
that was what happened.

Stacey stopped talking.
Started crying.

The door slammed again.
More yelling. Crashing sounds.
Silence.

20
The door opened.
Darra's voice:
Stay out here tonight.

He won't hurt you if you stay out of his way.
I bet you're hungry. Here's some food and water.

The door closed.

    (Who was she talking to?
    Does she know I'm here?)

Someone (Darra?) was in the garage.
    Moving around . . .
    coming closer . . .
        Right in the boat with me!
        I yelped! I couldn't help it.
    Yeeooowww.
A cat!
    Scratching my face. Barely missing my eye.
        We looked at each other.

    Carefully, I reached out to pet it.
        After a while, we both calmed down.
            It curled up in my arms and purred.

READ THE KAREN HESSE NOVELS
AVAILABLE FROM SQUARE FISH

LETTERS FROM RIFKA

Rifka knows nothing about America when she flees from Russia with her family in 1919. But she dreams she will be safe there from the Russian soldiers' harsh treatment of the Jews. On her long journey Rifka must endure a great deal: humiliating examinations, deadly typhus, murderous storms at sea, and separation from all she has ever known and loved. And even if she does make it to America, she's not sure America will have her.

ISBN-13: 978-0-312-53561-2
$6.99 US / $7.99 Can

WISH ON A UNICORN

Mags wishes she could live in a nice house with a mama who isn't tired out from work. She'd like a sister who's normal and a brother who doesn't mooch for food. And once in a while she'd like some new clothes for school. Then her sister finds a stuffed unicorn, and Mags's wishes start to come true. She knows the unicorn can't really be magic, but she's not going to let anything ruin her luck— even if it means believing something that can't possibly be true.

ISBN-13: 978-0-312-37611-6
$6.99 US / $7.99 Can

PHOENIX RISING

Nyle's quiet life with her grandmother on their farm is shattered the night of the accident at the nuclear power plant. Nyle's world fills with disruptions, protective masks, contaminated food, and mistrust. Things become even more complicated when "refugees" from the accident take shelter in Nyle's house. But Nyle doesn't want to open her heart to them. Too many times she's let people in, only to have them desert her. If she lets herself care, she knows they'll end up leaving her, too.

ISBN-13: 978-0-312-53562-9
$6.99 US / $7.99 Can

SQUARE FISH
WWW.SQUAREFISHBOOKS.COM
AVAILABLE AT YOUR LOCAL BOOKSTORE